VOLUME ONE
BONDAGE ENTHUSIASTS
BOUND IN LEATHER
ILLUSTRATED WITH 35 DRAWINGS BY STANTON
AF256103

BONDAGE ENTHUSIASTS

BOUND IN LEATHER

A Nutrix BOOK THAT IS BOUND TO PLEASE

VOLUME ONE

ILLUSTRATED WITH 35

DRAWINGS BY STANTON

RESTORED EDITION BY

EROSETTI PRESS

Erosetti Press

Let us journey, together

EROSETTIPRESS.COM

ISBN 978-1-968703-24-0 | COPYRIGHT 2026 EROSETTI PRESS

Introduction to the Restored Edition

Born Ernest Stanzoni Jr. in Brooklyn, New York on September 30, 1926, Eric Stanton discovered his muse early. By age twelve he was already tracing comic-book heroines—especially strong, commanding female figures like Wonder Woman and Sheena. That early fascination with powerful women who dominated the frame would shape everything that followed. After serving in the Navy during World War II—where he drew aircraft recognition strips for service newspapers and sketched glamorous girls on sailors' handkerchiefs—he suffered a head injury that left him partially color-blind. That limitation, some say, sharpened his bold black-and-white style with its dramatic shadows, emphatic outlines, and graphic force. Post-war, he assisted newspaper strip cartoonist Gordon "Boody" Rogers on Sparky Watts, learning the full craft of professional comics. He later enrolled at the Cartoonists and Illustrators School in the mid-1950s, where he shared a studio with a young Steve Ditko, the future co-creator of Spider-Man.

But Stanton's real passion always lay in the shadows. Hired by Irving Klaw at Nutrix Company in the late 1940s, he began illustrating the mail-order bondage serials that would make him underground royalty. Klaw encouraged him toward tighter ropes, higher heels, and stronger women. Stanton delivered in spades. His work evolved from "fighting femmes" into full theatrical bondage, domination, and power reversal. His art exploded with the themes that still define fetish today: fierce female dominance, corseted amazons, helpless men tamed by "Tame-Azons," gleaming leather, lace, forced feminization, theatrical humiliation, costume-as-fate, and unapologetic power exchange. He called it his private kingdom—"a world of which I am king."

Stanton occupies a strange and important place in American visual culture: famous in his niche, hugely influential beyond it, and yet still obscure enough that even now he is often discussed in fragments, half-myths, and collector lore. He was one of the major architects of an underground visual world built around female dominance, theatrical power reversal, costume, peril, humiliation, transformation, and stylized submission. Long before the internet made niche direct-to-consumer art publishing normal, Stanton was already working in a

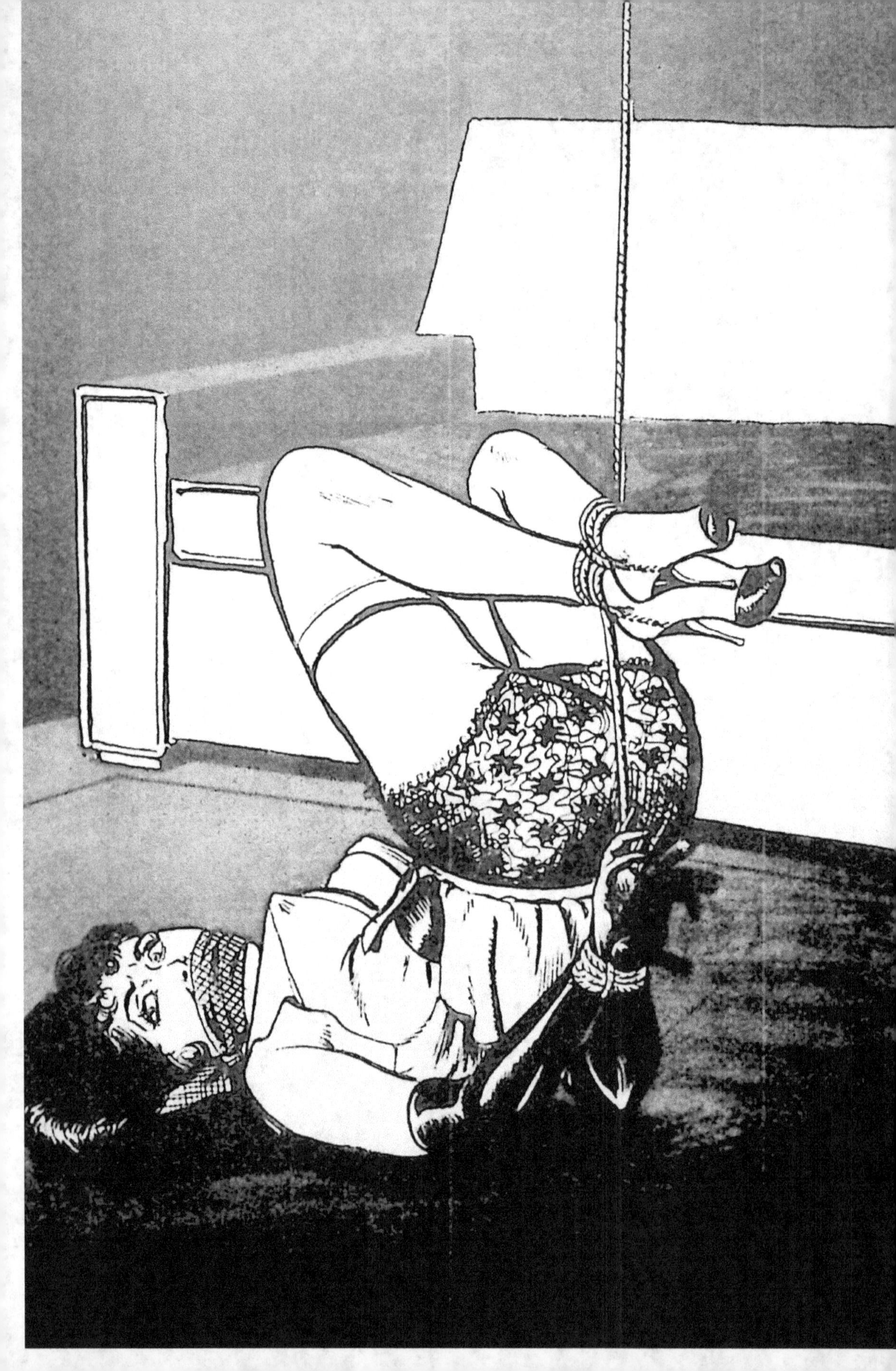

mode that modern independent erotic artists and small presses would immediately recognize: highly specific work for a devoted subculture, sold directly to enthusiasts, often outside mainstream approval, and sustained through a tight relationship between creator, collector, and fantasy. The Guardian's obituary called him "America's most provocative and influential post-war illustrator of bondage and domination," and that remains one of the better concise descriptions of his place in the culture.

At the height of his career his steely-eyed dominatrixes graced paperback covers (he painted around 300 of them), influenced Madonna's early look, and even caught the eye of collectors rumored to include Elvis and Howard Hughes. British painter Allen Jones praised his "expressionist intensity," pictorial invention, draughtsmanship, and humor. Yet Stanton stayed proudly underground—no mainstream fame, just a devoted following that kept him drawing for more than fifty years. On March 17, 1999, at age 72, the father of modern fetish art passed away, but his ink never faded.

Bondage Enthusiasts Bound in Leather, Volume One—is pure mid-century Stanton at his most elegant and extreme. First released by Nutrix in 1961, it follows a chance theater encounter that draws the narrator into the private world of Vicki Roberts and her daughter Nicki: sky-high heels that force every step into helpless mincing, wasp-waist corsets that crush the breath from a girl's lungs, gleaming kid-leather gloves and single-sleeved sheaths that pin arms into perfect, useless arches, and women who crave their own delicious captivity. The story is a masterclass in 1960s fetish theater—sophisticated, ritualized, and utterly unapologetic.

Erosetti Press is proud to present the first-ever Restored Edition. We meticulously cleaned and proofed the rare Nutrix printing, including 35 original drawings and two Nutrix advertisement pages that appeared in the first edition—those wonderful, long-lost pages of mail-order fetish ephemera that collectors have sought for decades. The volume is printed on premium archival paper with a glossy collectible cover. Whether you are a longtime Stanton collector or discovering him for the first time, welcome to Stanton's private fetish kingdom.

Dante Remy | Erosetti Press

ALL NEW ILLUSTRATED PHOTO STORY BOOKS!

"LETTERS FROM FEMALE IMPERSONATORS"

Volume One—"Letters From Female Impersonators" contains actual letters from amateur female impersonators who reveal in their correspondence interesting personal impressions about themselves and how they practice female impersonation. They tell why they would like to be accepted as females instead of men and the reasons for their preference for feminine clothes. Illustrated with 32 photos of men in women's clothes and sells for $3.75 each plus 20¢ for postage. Volumes 2, 3, also contains 32 photos and sells for $3.75 each plus postage of 20¢. These amateur impersonators tell how they obtain their female attire, what their desires are, how they first started to dress in clothing of the opposite sex and how they fool people into thinking that they are girls. three $3.75 books for only $10.00 postpaid.

"THE ART OF FEMALE IMPERSONATION"

reveals the secrets of how men become Female Impersonators and contains 32 actual photographs of men in "girls" attire. "The art of Female Impersonation" reveals the inner secrets of how men are transformed into girls with the aid of wigs, falsies, cosmetics and corsets. You will meet four pleasant young men who will let you peek behind the scenes as they make up for their amazing transformation into four lavishly gowned "women."

You see this all happen in 32 actual photographs as they create the changes from flat-chested men into the utmost in femininity. They tell how they became female impersonators — see the tricks they use to fool the public and how they effect cleavage. Volumes 1, 2, 3, 4, and 5 now available at $3.75 each plus 20¢ postage, or all five books for only $16.00 postpaid.

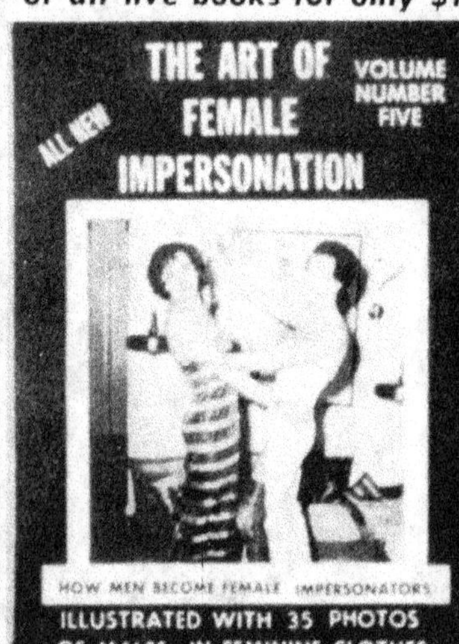

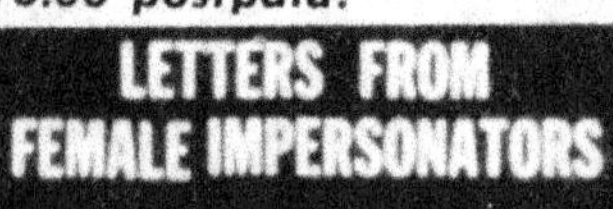

"FEMALE IMPERSONATORS ON PARADE"

Now available are volumes 1, 2, and Three on "Female Impersonators On Parade," which explain in detail the art of female impersonation or cross-dressing by men by the amateur and professional female impersonators themselves. You will have to have a very keen eye when looking at the "girls" for the men look more like girls than real girls do. Volume One contains 31 actual photographs, volume Two contains 45 real photos and volume Three contains 35 actual photos of glamour girls who are men. These books sell for $3.75 each volume plus 20¢ for postage.

"MORE FEMME MIMICS"

You will see professional Female Impersonators Jackie Jackson, Nicki Gallucci and others start dressing up in female clothes from the skin out. They explain about their experiences while transforming from male to alluring female clothing. Book contains 115 photos and sells for only $3.75 per copy plus 20 cents for postage. "More Femme Mimics" is book Two and you can also purchase book One "Femme Mimics," which contains 200 other different photos of female impersonators and retails for $3.75 each plus postage.

You may purchase any three of our $3.75 books for only $10.00 postpaid. Illustrated Model Photo Bulletin showing over 75 poses only 25 cents or five different illustrated bulletins for $1.00. Send all orders to

NUTRIX CO. Dept. 4-FM, 35 Montgomery St., Jersey City 2, N. J.

BONDAGE ENTHUSIASTS BOUND IN LEATHER

She appeared to be in her early thirties and completely feminine. We were both attending one of New York's hit straight comedies and I filled in most of the time by taking as much stock of my neighbor as I could without being too obvious.

About medium height, very slim at the waist, and her pretty face was positively striking. Her costume was conservative. She was clothed in clinging black satin, from a high, close-fitting collar, right down to a rather full, floor-length skirt. While in no sense tight, the shining black material was so subtly draped that it showed the lovely figure beneath it very clearly.

The long sleeves were full to the elbow and fitted snuggly down to the wrists, where they gave way to obviously extremely tight black kid gloves.   Long gold and ruby drop earrings, a close fitting necklace of the same design and a single gold ring, worn outside her right glove, completed the effect.

Very striking she was too, and I was by no means the only one looking at her. Something else that intrigued me was the way she sat. She held herself bold upright, hands on her lap, knees modestly together, still as a statue. She did not seem to be with the party of four next to her.

BONDAGE ENTHUSIASTS BOUND IN LEATHER

The approach to make her acquaintance had to be suble as she did not seem to be the type to you you can simply say, "Hey, how about a drink after the show." Suddenly I had an idea so I took a pencil and began sketching her boots on the margin of my program.

I paused thoughtfully and to my surprise she leaned toward me and murmured, "May I see it?"

"See what?" I asked in feigned astonishment. "The picture of me," she said.

"How do you know it's of you?" I asked.

"If it isn't, I've been wasting a lot of time posing," she dimpled. Naturally, I handed it over although it was unfinished.

"May I do that part?" She added some deft strokes, though the tightness of her gloves made it hard to hold the pencil. By this time, the curtain was going up so we had to give our attention to the play. The high point of this act and the real reason I had come was the kidnapping scene. The action took place in a night club run, naturally, by gangsters.

The heroine, the heiress to a large fortune, was working at the night club for some typical

comedy reason, as a cigarette girl and the chief gangster's girl was also working there in the same capacity. The chief gangster falls for the heroine and decides that her money would come in handy too.

He lures her into his office, ties her hands behind her, gags her with a knotted handkerchief and, to prevent her seeing where he is going to take her, he pulls a black sack over her head and down to her hips. He then gets a phone call and has to leave.

With her pretty legs in the mesh stockings of her calling, being all of her that was showing, I thought the heroine looked most attractive. Suddenly, the hero, who has been working at the club as a bartender, appears and frees the heroine, explaining that he had sent the fake phone call.

Hero and heroine are about to leave when the other girl busts in, looking for her gangster boy-friend. With one accord, hero and heroine jump on her, tie and gag her in the same way that the heroine had been treated, pull the sack down over her head and body in the same way and leave. The gangster's moll does some very pretty struggling and squirming, trying to escape, and also showing her very pretty legs.

The gangster returns, breathing threats against whoever sent the phone call. He begins to tell the helpless occupant of bag just how he proposes to treat her up at his little hide-away in the country. Much to his surprise, the legs show every indication of liking the things he suggests (of course, Moll has been trying to get him to do these things to her for years).

The more he threatened, the more the legs expressed approval. So he began embroidering his threats and her legs began to show a series of bumps and grinds. The gangster then realized that the heroine would not know how to do a bump or a grind but his girl had been in burlesque for years.

He tears the sack off and when he sees who it is, storms out saying, "Even without the sack, you're still an old bag!" This throws her into a perfect rage. Fruitlessly, the helpless girl tries to open the door, puts her high heel through the window to get help and finally knocks the phone off the cradle and as the curtain comes down, we see her trying to dial for help with her nose!

I remarked to my companion, "I thought that was terrific, didn't you?"

Slanton

"It was pretty funny but I would have liked it better if that had been a real gag, " she answered. I suggested that we go to the bar for a drink instead of sitting in the hot theatre and she made me very happy by agreeing.

"Good evening, Mrs. Roberts, " the bar captain said and brought us to a booth. As we sat down, I said, "So you're Mrs. Roberts?"

"That's right, Mrs. Richard Roberts, happily married and mother of a daughter. " She then talked about her husband, who insists on high heels for her carriage, corsets for her figure, bondage to make her helpless and a gag to assure that silence which is a guarantee of assent.

"How about your daughter? Is she being brought up the same way?" I asked.

"She won't have it any other way. At times, she insists on such severe treatment that we're afraid she will do herself permanent injury." Mrs. Roberts then asked if I would like to meet her daughter. "If she's anything like you, I'd be delighted, " I said.

I accepted her invitation to visit her and on the way she told me her name was Vicki, her daughter's name was Nicki and her husband,

Dick, was a brokerage house manager who was away for business and that was why she had come to the theatre alone. We were soon in a cab, heading for an address uptown.

"Would you unlock the door please," she requested, "My gloves are so tight, it's difficult for me." I heard a pleasant, slightly French accented voice begin to speak as I followed her in:-

"Madame is back so soon? Surely, the play cannot be over. But of course not. Madame did not stay beyond the second act as that is when the interest ceases."

"Fifi, this is a new friend of mine. You may be seeing a good deal of him--his name is Mr. Walk." Fifi was worth a long stare. Actually about medium height, she appeared tall by reason of the slim six-inch heels on her pretty ankle-strap sandals of black patent leather, shackled at the wrists and ankles with dainty cuffs and chains.

Fifi was called away and I turned and in-spected the living room. Money, and plenty of it, was obvious in the furnishings. One of the most striking features was the number of photo-graphs, some on the walls and some placed on tables and occasional pieces.

BONDAGE ENTHUSIASTS BOUND IN LEATHER

One picture caught my eye. It was a girl's head in an old-fashioned traveling hood and she looked Vicki. The pose was modeled on the famous sequence in "Jamaica Inn" and the subject was gagged, though the fact was not too obvious because of the shadow that the cloak cast on the face.

Her mouth was almost wide open and very tightly packed with a large pad of cloth, while the band that crossed the face and circled the head, keeping the pad in place, went between the parted teeth and was obviously pulled very taut. The subject's wide open eyes, with a tear in the corner of one, looked at the observer with a mixture of fright and desire that was extremely interesting.

Another photograph nearby was just a pair of bound hands. They were crossed and bound behind the owner's back. They were tightly gloved in glistening black kid, which contrasted very sharply with the almost white cord that imprisoned them.

The cord, by the way it sank into the flesh, was drawn very tightly. There was a tremendous sense of tension in the rigidly held, almost claw-like fingers.

Stanton

BONDAGE ENTHUSIASTS BOUND IN LEATHER

Over the fireplace was a very large photographic enlargement and the subject was presumably Vicki. She was seated stiffly upright and her face looked straight at the viewer. She wore a light colored evening dress and appeared to be so tiny in the waist and so full at the bust, that it seemed obvious a retoucher had been at work.

Vicki's arms were drawn over the back of the chair and secured. They were drawn back so far that the elbows must have been very close together or actually in contact.   The gown was transparent and showed that the legs were tightly laced into thigh-boots carrying heels at least seven inches high. The pretty ankles were strapped together and loops ran from the ankle bondage to each of the front legs of the chair.

Vicki was wearing a concealed gag; that is, the upper part of her face was free but her mouth was apparently packed with a pad that held her jaws about an inch apart. Then, from the root of the nose to the base of the chin her face was smoothly covered with something concealed and sealed the mouth. It may have gone all around the head. Finally, a pair of lips were painted in the proper position. It was a picture to delight a bondage lover's heart.

Another photograph, in color, fascinated me a lot. The subject was quite obviously Vicki and she wore a pair of marvelously fitting over-knee boots in flesh-colored leather, with about 8-inch heels. From boot-tops to waist she wore a pair of nude elastic mesh tights. From the waist to just below the jutting bust she had on a tiny waisted, stiffly boned corset of leather to match the boots.

Her arms were in tight flesh-colored leather gloves, which were joined to each other in such a manner that each hand was clasped around the opposite elbow. Thus, she was incapable of defending herself. Her mouth was drawn far back at the corners into a fixed grin by a narrow band of the same leather drawn very tightly between her teeth, and presumably buckled behind her head. Her mouth was packed with some sort of silencing pad.

There were other pictures in the room but we will not take the time to describe them all. Suddenly I heard Vicki's voice, "Will you open the door, please?" I hastened to oblige, wondering why she could not open it herself. She minced past me, holding herself very upright and taking very small steps and as she passed, I saw the reason for her upright pose.

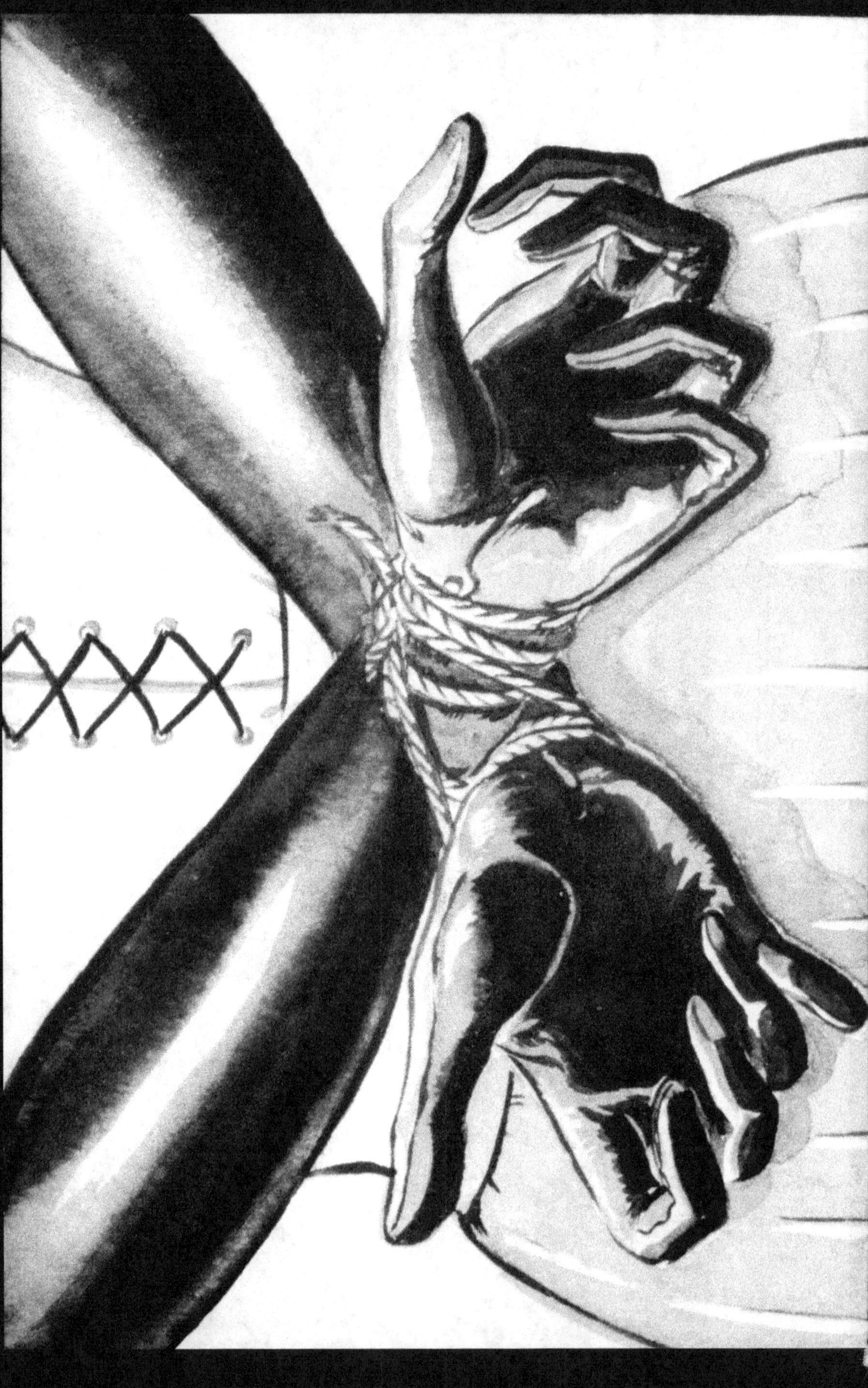

Her arms were held behind her back in a "Y" shaped glove of black kid.   It reached almost to the arm-pits and the two separate arms joined into one at the elbows, which were held in actual contact in the small of her back.   From there, down to the tips of her fingers, it was a single glove, holding her forearms, hands and even fingers rigidly together.

"Well?" she smiled, "How do I look?"

From a very low-cut bust-line down to her toes, she was wearing a skin-tight gown of what I took to be raspberry red velvet.   It fitted her like a skin.   The bones of her corset, the tops and lacing of her boots were all clearly outlined. Suddenly I realized that her bosom, incredibly high and full, must tape well over forty inches, while her wasp waist could not have been any more than eighteen inches.

"Well?" she pouted, "Aren't you going to say anything?"

"So that's what you meant by the figure you wear in public!" I exclaimed.   She strutted over to a straight chair and asked, "Aren't you going to say that I look pretty?"

"Well, frankly, " I replied, "I've never seen anybody like you before.   I've heard that there

"Why, no, I don't think so. Thank you, Fifi,"
I said.

As Fifi left, Vicki asked her, "Fifi, where's
Miss Nicki?"

"She spent most of the day in the dark-room,
madame, working on those last pictures. But
she came out and told me she had been very
clumsy. Her high heel had turned and she had
spilled some solution. She wanted to be pun-
ished."

Vicki nodded and asked, "How did you punish
her?"

"I locked her in the trunk, madame."

"Good," said Vicki. "Well, in about ten
minutes, bring her up here. I want her to meet
Mr. Walk."

"Oui, madame.   Still in the trunk?"

"I don't see why not. Maybe Mr. Walk
would like taking her out of it."   This was all
Greek to me, but I resolved not to say anything.
If they wanted to regard this punishing of girls
by putting them in trunks as a natural thing to
do, I was not going to be any different.   Instead,
I stepped over to the tray and picked out a long
piece of rather heavy rope.

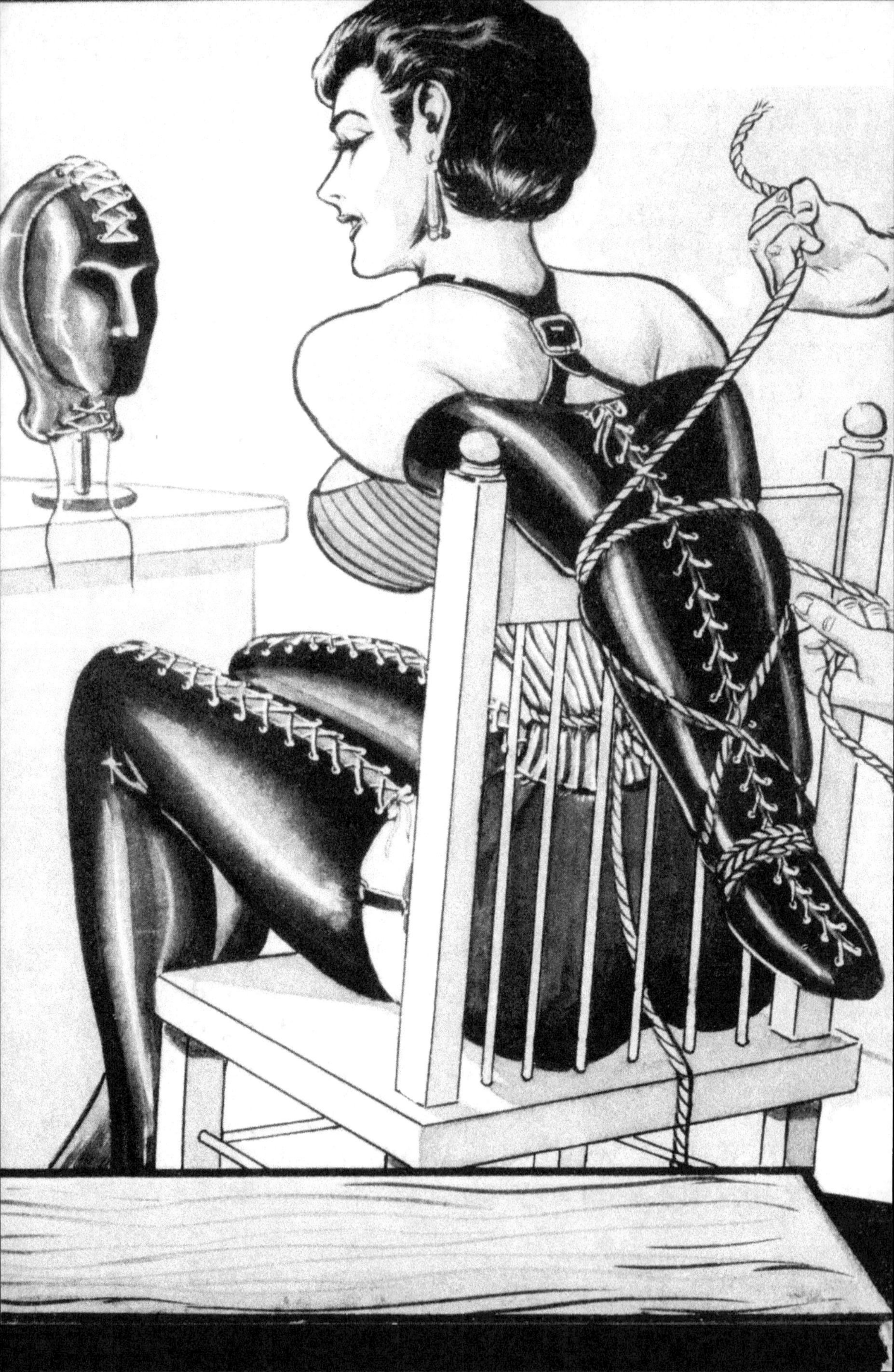

Fifi then minced over to the door and departed. I beckoned my willing victim over, passed the rope once around her pretty little waist and tied it firmly at the back, with two long ends equal and trailing almost to the floor. Then I helped her to sit in the chair, well back in the seat, with her gloved arms over the back. I brought the two ends of the rope forward, one around each side.   Then I passed them back under her body.

Next I tied a shorter rope, figure of eight wise, several times around her upper arms, just above the elbows.   I brought the two ends of the rope from under her body up through the arm rope and pulled it as tightly as I could. The result was to pull her shoulders back and down, make her arch her back as much as her stiff corset would allow.

"Oh!" she gasped softly, as the rope drew tight, "That feels wonderful. I can see I'm going to enjoy this. I love it."

I tied a short rope to each pretty ankle, passed the ropes outside the front legs of the chair and back underneath to her gloved wrists. Pulling these short ropes very tightly, I forced her legs wide apart in front then, bent steeply at the knees, with the toes well clear of the floor,

back under the seat.   I then secured the ropes
around her wrists.

"Have you ever done this sort of thing before?" asked Vicki and I answered, "Well,
once or twice and only in fun."

"I must say you seem to have a natural knack
for it.   I feel delightfully helpless."   Feeling
highly complimented, I continued to secure her.
I passed a long strap, figure of eight wise, around her upper body and the back of the chair and
pulled it extremely tight across her chest, above
and below her bosom.   Two more shorter straps
went around each knee, anchoring them securely
to the front legs of the chair.

"I now feel like a trussed chicken," she
smiled.   Suddenly there was a knock at the door
and Fifi's voice spoke, "Here is Miss Nicki,
madame."

I saw a small dark green trunk, up on one
end, supported by a pair of singularly, lovely
legs in dark brown thigh-boots.   Guided by Fifi,
this vision strutted into the room, taking steps
not much over six inches long.   The extremely
thin heels on the boots were over eight inches
high, but each pace, though tiny, was perfect—
not a trace of a tremor at the ankles, the knees

quite straight and firm, the rounded toes of the beautifully fitting boots being pointed so far down that the walk was entirely on the toes, the heels touching the ground only when the occupant of the boots stood still.

Her walk was light as thistledown and very reminiscent of a ballet dancer moving on tip-toe. The trunk was just large enough to enclose a girl from the top of her head to the fork of her legs, allowing just enough width for her shoulders.

Fifi sort of aimed her in the general direction of Vicki's chair and Vicki said, "Nicki, dear, can you hear me?" The trunk bowed slightly. "Did Fifi tell you about what I did tonight?" The trunk pivoted back and forth in what was obviously a movement of "No."

"While I was at the theatre, I sat next to a very nice young man. He is here to meet you, also. In fact, he has tied me up on this chair. If you want to say "Hello" to him, he's just to the right of me here." The trunk turned in my direction and the legs did a very nice curtsey. Fifi then stepped forward and asked, "May Fifi make a suggestion, madame?"

"Certainly, Fifi, what is it?" said Vicki.

"Perhaps you and Monsieur Walk would like some coffee? Miss Nicki would make a lovely coffee table."

Casually, Fifi took a corner of the trunk and maneuvered Nicki around so that she stood sideways to Vicki. I then helped to place the trunk down gently, with Nicki's pretty legs sticking out of it. The lock side of the trunk was toward Vicki and the clasps and lock were securely closed. Her legs, which thrust through two holes cut on one end, were set off by the skin fitting brown boots that laced very tightly from toe-cap to the top of the leg.

The heels came down to bases smaller than a dime, while the bearing part of the sole was not much over an inch, allowing no more than the first joints of the toes to touch the ground. Fifi brought in the tray, making a very pretty picture in her own right, with her lovely corsetted figure in gleaming black satis, contrasting so sharply with the mesh-covered legs and sandalled feet on their six-inch spindle heels.

I poured two cups of coffee and then Fifi returned, carrying a nickel plated metal bar, about four feet long, with an ankle cuff at each end. Nick's ankles were locked at the cuffs, her legs spread wide apart.

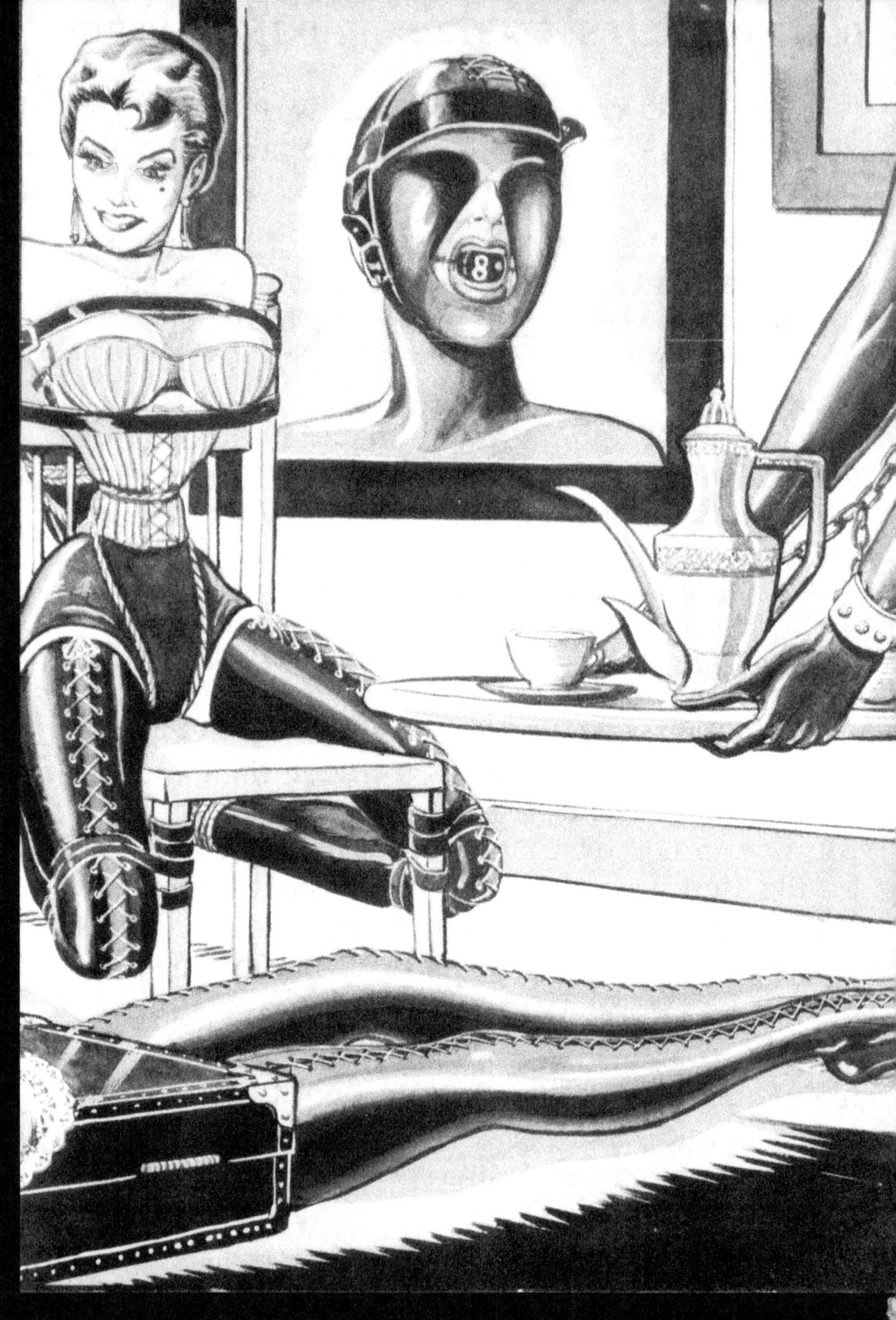

BONDAGE ENTHUSIASTS BOUND IN LEATHER

"I know how impatient you are to unlock that trunk, " Vicki smiled. "I guess you'd better begin the grand opening by taking the coffee and things off the trunk. Better unlock that leg stretcher and take it off next. You'd have a tough job getting her out of the trunk with that in place, since she couldn't help you." I obeyed her instructions and the pretty legs began moving and twisting about, gently at first, then more freely.

"Getting the kinks out, " Vicki explained. "That position gets very uncomfortable in a few minutes." Using the key, I unlocked the main clasp and opened the ones at each end. My heart beating with excitement, I threw back the lid. But instead of a face, I saw a mask in flesh-colored suede. It was skin tight and fitted the contours beneath it without a wrinkle.

The eye-holes were little more than narrow slits, turned up at the outer corners and fringed with long artificial lashes of black. Thin brows of black arched above them and the eye lid area was even shadowed in green. There were touches of rouge on the high, prominent cheek bones. The hair was represented by a wig of stiffened silk fringe. The faintly smiling lips, in deep red, were made of a piece of colored kid, sewn in the proper place.

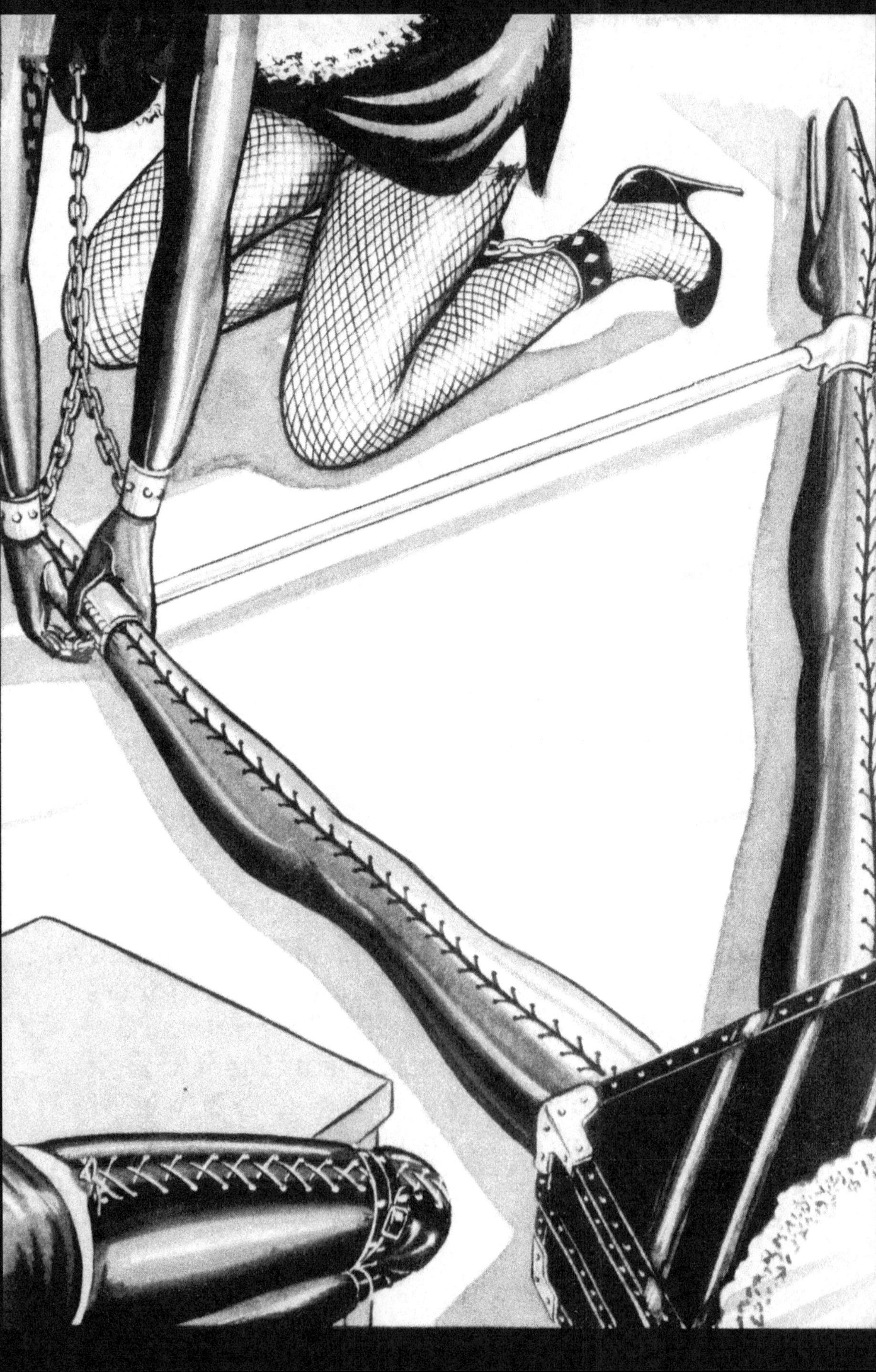

The arms, tightly gloved in gleaming black kid, right up to the shoulders, where they were met by very brief but side sleeves on the blouse, were folded and tightly strapped to rest in the corsetted arch of the small of the back.

"Nicki must be an utter and complete bondage enthusiast," I said in amazement.

"Oh, yes," Vicki agreed. "I'm pretty strong in that line myself, but Nicki wears costumes, insists on bondage and silencers that would make me a wreck." I quickly bent over and unfastened the straps that held her so tightly bound in the trunk.

The trunk was such a tight fit and her costume so stiff, that I puzzled for a moment as to how to get her out. Telling her to hold herself rigid, I lifted behind her wigged head with my left hand and when she was clear of the trunk, I slipped my other one behind her waist and continued lifting. In a second, she was upright, poised on the tips of her toes and her towering heels.

Nicki stepped back a little, spun lightly on her heels and presented her rigidly strapped arms. "What does she want now" I asked. "To have me unstrap her arms?"

"Probably, under the circumstances--but you'd better ask her," Vicki answered. "It's quite possible that she simply wants the straps tightened."

"Well?" I asked the intriguing figure, "shall I take the straps off?" She nodded, moving even closer to me. When I took them off I was surprised that she had full use of her arms immediately, even though the straps had been so tight. Turning to face me and stepping back a foot or two, she placed her gloved hands on her tiny waist, put her feet together and posed for my approval. She looked utterly delightful.

Then, with surprising quickness and grace, Nicki minced over to the bondage material, picked up a big wad of absorbent cotton and a roll of adhesive tape and started for where her mother sat, helplessly tied to her chair.

"Nicole, I will not allow you to gag me. Put that stuff back immediately!" It was just as though Vicki had not spoken, for all the attention her daughter paid. Nicki motioned me to help her and Vicki pleaded, "Ted, you'll listen to me, won't you? You won't let her gag me, will you?"

"You're damn right I will!" I grinned heartily. "Your lovely daughter has impressed me

so much with her charming silence, that I'm convinced, lovely as you are, you'll be lovelier yet with a gag in your mouth."

"Well, try to get it in!" snapped the helpless woman, writhing fruitlessly in her chair and she clamped her jaws tightly together. This would have presented quite a problem, since the jaw muscles are enormously strong. However, her daughter was serenly confident. She passed behind Vicki's chair, beckoned me to stand in front and gave me the wad of cotton, gesturing that I should compress it as small as possible.

Nicki placed her thumbs against her mother's cheeks then placed her first fingers, one against each nostril, and pressed gently. Result--no air through the nose. In a few seconds, Vicki countered by parting her lips in a sort of grin, breathing between her clenched teeth. The tightly gloved hands met this challenge by closing over the mouth, while also keeping the nostrils closed!

Vicki fought but had no chance--she gave in and opened her mouth. Her daughter removed her fingers but thrust in with her thumbs so that her victim could not close her mouth without biting her cheeks and nodded to me to pack the cotton in place.

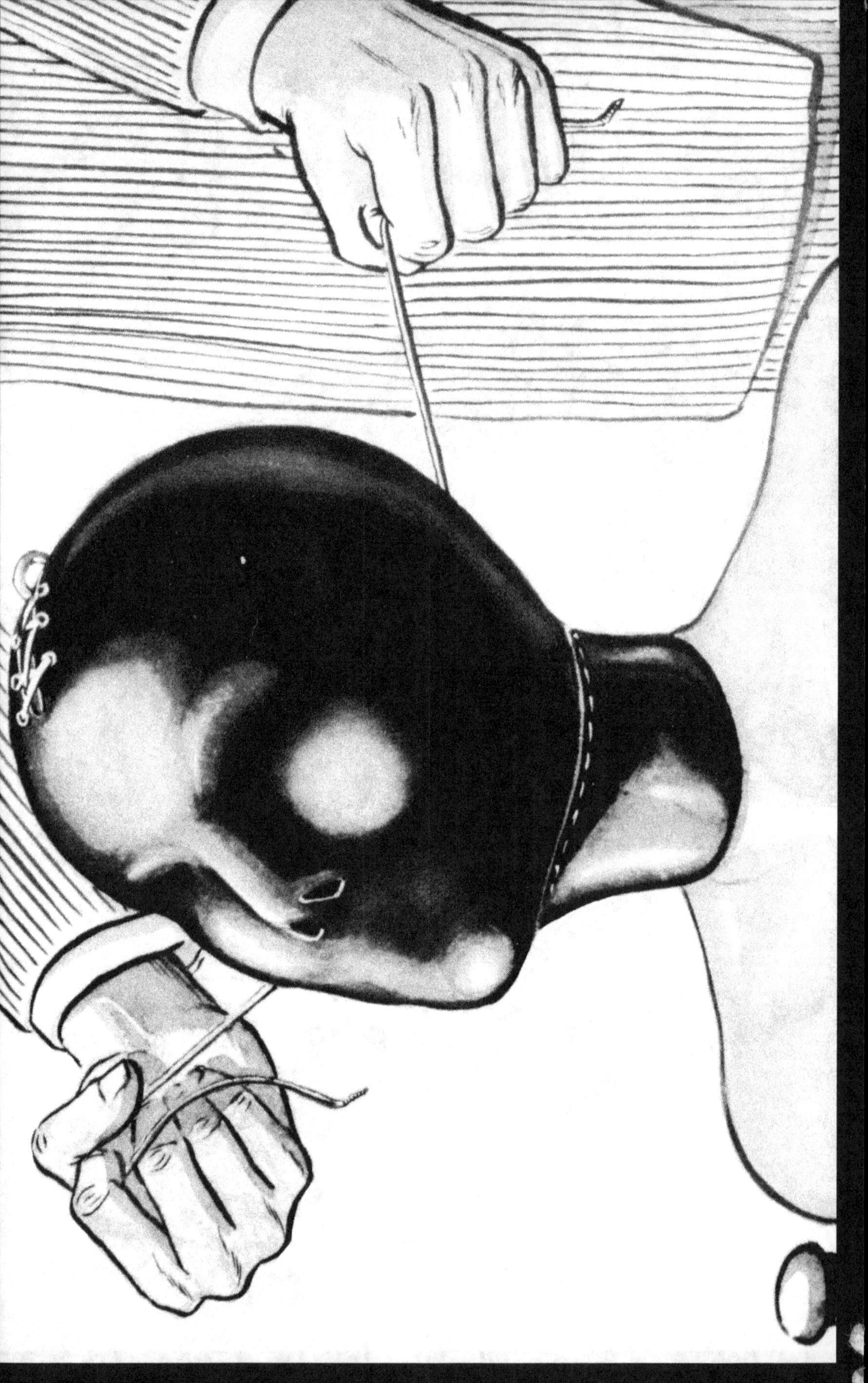

This was a delightful job for me. I had never gagged a woman before but could now see that I had missed a treat.   When I had her mouth packed full, I paused and asked the silent figure behind our victim, "Isn't that enough?"

Nicki shook her head. "Well, how much more?" I asked. "Surely, not all of it!"

Nicki nodded.   Even though she could not see her, her helpless victim sensed her daughter's answer and moaned faintly.   Eager to oblige, I got all the cotton stuffed into my subject's gaping mouth.   Nicki was tearing off a piece of adhesive tape a little over two feet long and placed the center of the tape on the cotton as it bulged between her victim's teeth, brought the ends back along her cheeks and got ready to pull them tight.

The way she did this startled me.   Nicki actually placed a knee against the back of her mother's neck and pulled with all her might! Poor Vicki writhed convulsively and her eyes flew open in anguish but so tight was the gag, that she could not utter the least sound.   Nicki removed her knee and lapped the ends. She took the roll of tape and passed the adhesive three times completely around her head and through her mouth.

BONDAGE ENTHUSIASTS BOUND IN LEATHER

Vicki had a look of obvious pain but there was also a look of very definite excitement on her face. Apparently satisfied, Nicki walked around and stood a few feet away from her mother, admiring her handiwork. She then picked up some vague black leather shape, which turned out to be a discipline helmet, and motioned for me to put it on her mother.

It took a moment or two to figure how it went on. It was heavily padded over the ears and made the victim "deaf, dumb and blind." The helmet was a beautiful piece of work, fitting the wearer's head like a skin. Nicki helped me lace and smooth out the helmet. Vicki's silent, helpless head looked almost like a portrain head in ebony.

One thing that had puzzled me was a metal eyelet sewn to the exact top of the head. I understood the use of this when Nicki took a piece of rope and signaled to me to tie it around Vicki's ankles. Then she took the other end and passed it through the eyelet and began pulling. Vicki's head was drawn back until I thought her neck must break. With a pretty gesture, after she tied the rope, Nicki stepped back and made a feint of dusting her gloved hands off.

BONDAGE ENTHUSIASTS BOUND IN LEATHER

It seemed to me that it was time for me to make some contribution to the proceedings so, pointing to the trunk lying open on the floor, I suggested, "It seems a shame to leave that empty. Do you think that we could squeeze Fifi into it?"

Nicki nodded and clapped her tightly gloved hands in eager agreement. She minced quickly to the tray of bondage materials and selected a gag consisting of a wide leather strap, about 18 inches long. At the middle it was narrower for an inch or two and on this was strung a leather egg, about two inches in diameter and three inches long.

Nicki rang the bell and in a few seconds we heard the crisp tap of Fifi's high heels. "Did mam'selle--ulb!" was all she managed to say, as I slipped in back of her, grabbed her elbows and pinned them behind her, the chain between her wrists drawing taut and securing her hands.

Nicki slapped the gag hard against her lips. The egg was so big, she had to push hard to force it between her squirming victim's teeth. But she got it in and quickly drew the strap as tightly as she could, stretching the corner's of Fifi's mouth back in a sort of fixed grin.

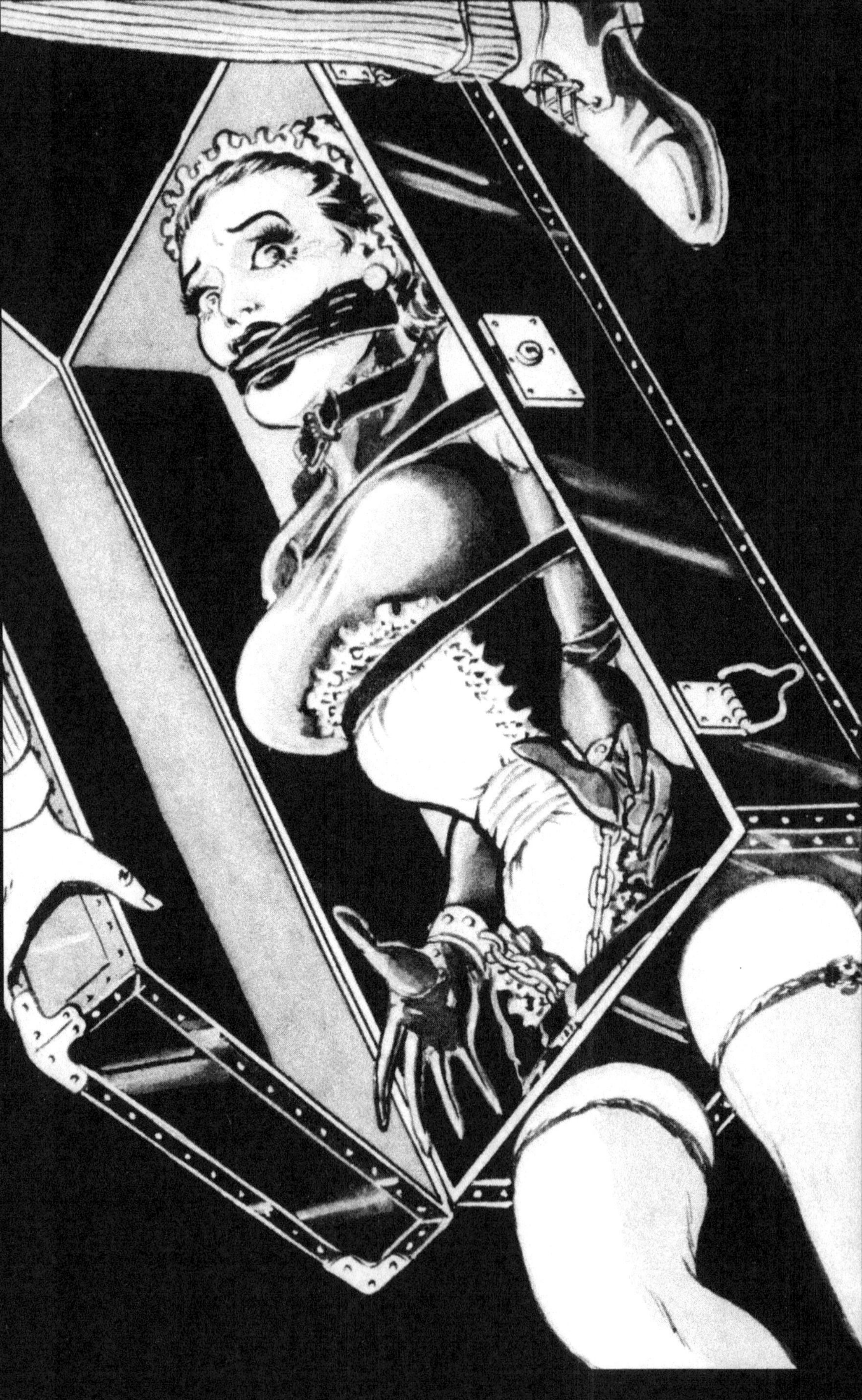

BONDAGE ENTHUSIASTS BOUND IN LEATHER

The expression on Fifi's face was a blend of surprise, pain and excitement. My silent companion wound a strap a couple of times through Fifi's elbows and pulled it tight. She released the chain that ran from wrist-chain to collar, passed it under the maid's body and pulled it up and fastened it to the strap around her elbows. Nicki then took a strap about 3 inches wide and passed it around Fifi's head and across her gaping mouth, lacing it closed at the back of her head.

Then, upon Nicki's signal, I put the captive into the trunk. Since Fifi was a bit larger in the body than Nicki, I had quite a lot of pleasant difficulty in wedging her into the trunk. Her pretty legs kicked and flailed delightfully as I pulled the anchoring straps tightly, so that from the hips up she had not the least power of movement. As I closed the lid, I took a last long look at her lovely helpless figure, silent face and eloquent eyes begging mutely for relief.

Fifi was now a pretty package, ready for shipment to Vicki's country home. The only problem remaining for us was how to transport her to the country, where she was to act as our chaperon. This remained to be seen.

THE END

ALL NEW ILLUSTRATED PHOTO STORY BOOKS!

LISTED BELOW ARE SOME OF OUR PUBLICATIONS, EACH CONTAINING 64 PAGES
AND SELLING FOR ONLY $3.75 EACH, PLUS 20 CENTS POSTAGE AND HANDLING:

Arduous Figure Training At Bondhaven
Art of Female Impersonation —
   Volumes 1, 2, 3, 4, 5
Beautiful Fighting Girls (BETTY PAGE)
Betty Page In Bondage—Volumes 1, 2, 3, 4, 5
Bondage Artist Dominated By Tame-Azons
Bondage Discipline At Bondhaven
Bondage Society's Bizarre Costume Ball
Bondage Sleuth's Harrowing Plight
Bondage Terror At Women's Prison
Bound In Rubber
Captive Slave's Dire Distress
Chained Captives In Bondageville
Chastised and Initiated Into Bondage Sorority
Disciplined Male Changed To Female
Dominant Whip Girls In High Heels —
   Volumes 1, 2
Dominated Man's Bondage Harassment
Dominating Woman Turns Man Into Girl

Fearful Ordeal In Restraintland
Female Impersonators On Parade —
   Volumes 1, 2, 3
Female Doctor Forced Into Bondage
Femme Mimics
Femme Mimic Tied By Dominant Woman
Girls Concentration Camp Torture Ordeals
Girl Psycho Handled With Restraint
Girls Punishment At School Of Discipline
Girls Reformatory Punishment
Girls Tied Up In Leather And Rubber
Inquisition At The Les Slaves Club
Kidnapped Girls Sweet Revenge
Letters From Female Impersonators —
   Volumes 1, 2, 3
Letters On Bondage Discipline
Male Captives Forced Into Female Attire
Manacled Slaves Bondage Adventures
Maria Stinger In Bondage — Volumes 1, 2

Men Made To Become Female Impersonators
Men Tamed To Submission By Tame-Azons
More Femme Mimics — Volume 2
New Adventures In Fetterland
Pleasure Parade — Volumes 1 and 6 only
Reporter Subdued By Domineering Girls
Return Visit To Fetterland
Shanghaied Slaves Cruise Of Horror
Subjugating A Male Bondage Model
Tales of Female Domination Over Man —
   Volumes 1, 2
Tame-Azons Subdue and Subjugate Man
Terror At The Bizarre Art Museum
Vacation in Fetterland (128 pages)
Women Bind and Dominate Male Maid
Women Enslave and Humiliate Author
Women In Distress — Volumes 2 and 3
Women of History Dominating Males

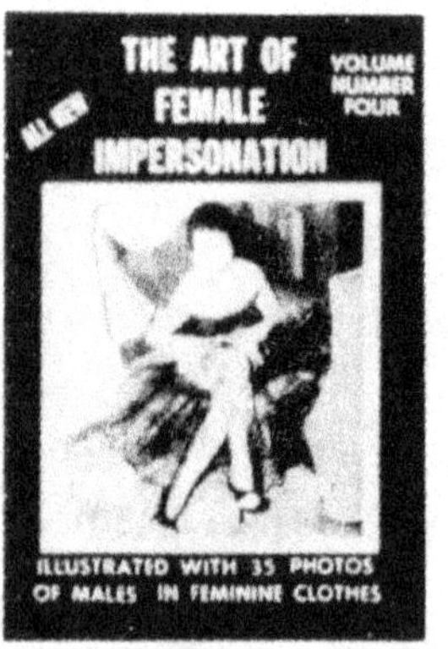

any 3 of our $3.75 books for only $10.00 postpaid.

NUTRIX CO. 35 Montgomery St., Jersey City 2, N. J.